PIZAZZ

Sophy Henn

ALADDIN

New York   London   Toronto   Sydney   New Delhi

ALADDIN

An imprint of Simon & Schuster Children's Publishing Division

1230 Avenue of the Americas, New York, New York 10020

First Aladdin hardcover edition June 2021

Copyright © 2020 by Sophy Henn. All rights reserved.

Originally published in Great Britain in 2020 by Simon & Schuster UK Ltd.

Also available in an Aladdin paperback edition.

All rights reserved, including the right of reproduction in whole or in part in any form.

ALADDIN and related logo are registered trademarks of Simon & Schuster, Inc.

For information about special discounts for bulk purchases, please contact Simon & Schuster Special Sales at 1-866-506-1949 or business@simonandschuster.com.

The Simon & Schuster Speakers Bureau can bring authors to your live event.

For more information or to book an event contact the Simon & Schuster Speakers Bureau at 1-866-248-3049 or visit our website at www.simonspeakers.com.

The illustrations for this book were rendered digitally.

The text of this book was set in New Clarendon MT.

Manufactured in the United States of America 0421 FFG

2 4 6 8 10 9 7 5 3 1

Library of Congress Cataloging-in-Publication Data

Names: Henn, Sophy, author, illustrator. | Title: Pizazz / Sophy Henn.

Description: [New York : Aladdin, 2021] | Series: Pizazz ; 1 | Originally published: London : Simon & Schuster, 2020. | Audience: Ages 8 to 10. | Summary: Nine-year-old superhero Pizazz relates how difficult it is to be a superhero, especially when, after moving to a new school, she is made "eco monitor" for her class. | Identifiers: LCCN 2020052003 (print) | LCCN 2020052004 (ebook) | ISBN 9781534492431 (hardcover) | ISBN 9781534492424 (paperback) | ISBN 9781534492448 (ebook) Subjects: CYAC: Superheroes—Fiction. | Middle schools—Fiction. | Schools—Fiction. | Ecology—Fiction. | Moving, Household—Fiction. Classification: LCC PZ7.H3912 Piz 2021 (print) | LCC PZ7.H3912 (ebook) | DDC [Fic]—dc23

LC record available at https://lccn.loc.gov/2020052003

LC ebook record available at https://lccn.loc.gov/2020052004

The bit about me . . .

Okay. Well, I am 9¼, almost 9½, and my name is **PIZAZZ**.

Yes, you did hear that right. My name is

PIZAZZ.

And yes, it IS completely embarrassing. And no, I don't think it's a proper name either, but as with most things around here, it really doesn't seem to matter what I think about it.

With a ridiculous name like **PIZAZZ**, I should probably be a **magician**, or a **POP STAR**, or a **really smelly perfume**, but I am not any of those things.

What I actually am is super. Not super as in brilliant, or terrific, or even very good. I am **SUPER** super. *Actually* super. As in superhero, with powers and stuff.

Because of this, I HAVE to wear a costume, and part of that costume is a very annoying cape. It gets in the way, flapping around my feet and trailing in puddles and getting stuck in doors, but I still have to wear it

ALL
THE
TIME.

Not just when it's cold.

Oh, and the best part . . . ?

. . . My ridiculous name (which in case you hadn't already guessed, I HATE) is written right across the back of my cape in **HUGE** shiny letters.

SUPER.

I come from a family of **_SUPERHEROES_**, which is generally how it works. Not always, I mean, there's the occasional freak accident in a scientist's lab or a weird weather/insect/reclusive millionaire "incident" that ends up with a perfectly normal person being able to climb up glass buildings or make

lightning or jump really, really, really high or suddenly talk in a low gravelly voice. But mainly you're just born and find yourself in a family of **SUPERHEROES** and you can fly and stuff. Then, if you are like me you might find yourself wondering why you don't feel quite as delighted about this as the rest of your family does.

MY *SUPER* FAMILY

The most annoying person in my family is definitely my little sister. She's like a **SUPERHERO** crossed with a **CHEERLEADER** crossed with someone who is completely good at everything. Oh, and did I mention she's really happy all the time? Well, she is.

Also, unlike me, she's actually got a cool superhero name . . . **RED DRAGON**.

Which is just ANOTHER of the many reasons I know my parents prefer her to me.

FIRST DAY AT ART CLASS...

THE MOLECULAR STRUCTURE OF CHOCOLATE

A HOUSE

FIRST SCHOOL SPORTS DAY...

ON YOUR MARKS, GET SET...

GOOOOOOOOOOOO...

...OH.

FIRST SCHOOL PLAY...

AUDITIONS

CAST LIST

ME

SEE WHAT I MEAN?

I call her **RED** for short because **RED DRAGON** is quite a mouthful to say if you just want someone to pass the TV remote, get a snack, or even GO AWAY. But she is absolutely **NOT** allowed to call me **PIZ**. If I am feeling generous, she can call me **ZAZZ**, but she is never really sure when I am actually feeling generous, and if I am honest neither am I, so she tends to just call me **PIZAZZ**. With a name like **RED DRAGON**, obviously her superpower

is that she can breathe **fire**, which is really useful, not just for defeating baddies but at barbecues, too, and for birthday cake candles. She's also got **SUPER SPEED**, which is okay, I suppose. They are both way cooler than my superpower, which is the least cool of all the superpowers, and in fact so uncool that sometimes I even consider letting the baddies win so I don't actually have to use it. Yes, it's THAT embarrassing. Anyway, I cannot even talk about it right now.

It's just all **SO** unfair.

My parents were sort of super famous about a million years ago because they have saved the word about a trillion times, but these days they just make me and RED do everything. Neutralize rockets, realign planets, load the dishwasher. It's like we are their personal servants or something.

And if you think it's hard to have your **mum** and **dad** cheering you on from the sidelines at sports day, try having them cheer you on while you and your irritating little sister divert a **planet-sized** meteor that's on a direct collision course with Earth. Yup. No pressure.

And, unlucky for me, it's not just my immediate family that is completely weird. Oh no. It's actually my entire family. . . .

Grandma
(Mum's mum)

Uncle Teaser
(Mum's little brother)

Uncle Titanooooooo
(Dad's little brother and yes, there are that many o's)

Gramps
(Mum's dad)

Red Dragon
(Annoying)

Mum

Dad

Me, duh

Grandmother
(Dad's slightly scary mum)

Aunty Fury
(Dad's sister who went to the dark side ... We don't talk about her much)

Wanda
(Not a pet)

Aunty Blaze
(Dad's AWESOME sister)

ALSO . . .

We have a dog. She's not exactly a pet dog, but more like a total bossy boots who happens to have four legs, a tail, flappy ears, and can't resist running after anything you throw. We call her **WANDA**, because that's her name, and she came to us from **MISSION CONTROL**, who are basically in charge of which super goes where, saves what, and when. So, instead of having an actual phone to talk to **MISSION CONTROL** like normal, sensible people, we have a dog who receives and transmits messages and generally keeps an eye on us. Although totally embarrassing and completely weird, it does actually work okay most of the time, though **WANDA** is absolutely **NOT** allowed to go on any missions anymore. This is because **Dad** threw one of DABOMB's super-scratchy itching powder bombs into outer space just before it exploded, but **WANDA** *zoomed off* and fetched it right back just in time for it to explode and make us all itch FOREVER. (Well, not quite forever, but at least a month.)

ROCKET

We also have two guinea pigs— well, I have one and my sister has the other. They are actual pets and don't do anything other than the usual guinea pig stuff, but they are still super. Just normal super, like great! My guinea pig is called **BERNARD**. I named it before I knew it was a girl, but it still really suited her and I think she likes it, so I stuck with it. My sister's guinea pig is called **ROCKET**, and is actually just as annoying as she is. They are both always *dashing* about, achieving stuff, and basically showing off. **BERNARD** is more laid-back, like me. We both like to sleep a lot, and eat a lot, too. And we have the same favorite snack: shrimp chips. Nice.

Most people seem to think that being a superhero must be completely wonderful. They are actually very wrong. You have probably guessed that I am not particularly thrilled with being **SUPER**, BUT there are a FEW good things about it. Just a few.

BERNARD

THINGS THAT ARE

SUP

① FLYING...

Obviously that is a great thing,* but not all superheroes can actually fly, i.e., my little sister. HAHAHAHAHAAAAAAA.

*I mean...FLYING!

2 HAVING A WHOLE FAMILY OF SUPERHEROES WHO ARE WATCHING OUT FOR YOU...

Aunty Sarah

Super but not *SUPER* super

Well, I say a whole family, but there is my aunty Sarah, and she's not actually a superhero. Well, not in the usual sense, though my **mum** says she should have a medal for putting up with *Uncle Teaser*.

She has a point. And then there's my *Aunty Fury*, who I am not supposed to talk about as she is now a **BADDIE**!!! **Shhhhhhhh.**

❸ YOU GET SUPERPOWERS...

This is normally a great thing, especially if your power is like

SUPER SPEED

OR

SUPERSTRENGTH

OR LASER EYES

. . . that can see through people and even buildings. But if you are me and have the worst, most awful, **embarrassing** *SUPERPOWER* in the universe, then it definitely belongs on the next list. . . . .

NOT SO SUPER . . .

There are waaaaaaaay more **STINKY** things about being a superhero. At least I think so. . . .

SCHOOL...

Even though I am a **SUPERHERO**, *whizzing* around saving a world or a town or a kitten from almost certain doom, I still have to go to school, which seems a bit much to me. **Mum** is ALWAYS **blah**, **blah**, **blahing** about how it's important to have something to fall back on just in case all the baddies decide to turn over a new leaf. As if! As far as I can work out, no matter how many baddies get defeated, there are just a million more lining up behind them to cause havoc with their fancy *LASER* blasters and snazzy **STINK-BOMB** makers.

❷ YOU HAVE TO WEAR THE SAME OUTFIT THE WHOLE TIME . . .

Well, we have lots of spares of the same outfit. I mean, we're not gross. Apart from **FARTERELLA**— **she really is gross**—but other than that, we are actually fairly hygienic.

❸ YOU ARE ALWAYS DISAPPEARING OFF TO SAVE ALL OF MANKIND...

One minute you are about to choose a delicious ice cream—*will it be banana-chocolate chip or toffee-chocolate chip or chocolate-chocolate chip?*—and the next minute you're zooming off on a mission. It can **REALLY** get in the way of stuff, and not just delicious ice creams.

Here are some examples of just how annoying it can be. . . .

4 ALL THAT DISAPPEARING MAKES IT REALLY HARD TO HAVE FRIENDS...

Despite this, I did actually have two of the best friends in the whole world, the universe even: **Tom** and **Susie**, at my old school. They never ever, ever got annoyed with me constantly disappearing. They never thought my cape was strange, and they didn't even mind about the *STINK JUICE*. I guess that's because I have known them my whole life and that's how things have always been—they were used to having a superhero best friend. Called **PIZAZZ**.

But now everything's changed because besides giving me the worst name ever AND a stupid cape, my parents decided they needed to ruin my life a bit more by making us move. In fact, not just to a new house, but to a whole new town, which is hard enough normally, but when you are a **super weirdo** like me, I am certain it is even harder. There's just so much to explain all the time. Maybe I should just get it all printed on a T-shirt. Or a cape. **Ha. Ha.**

AND THEN THERE'S . . .

5

YOU ALWAYS HAVE TO BE THE GOODIE, even when you don't feel like it.

6

THE WHOLE OF EARTH'S EXISTENCE DEPENDS ON YOU. Well, not JUST you, you and all the other superheroes . . . but sometimes just you if the others are busy with something else. And that can be quite a worry.

7

YOU SPEND A LOT OF YOUR TIME WISHING YOU WERE NORMAL. Well, at least I do.

The bit where I start a new school…

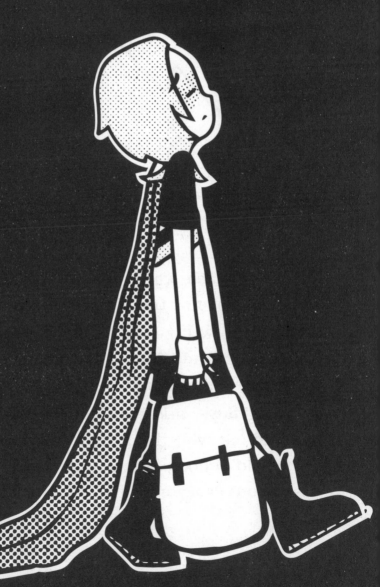

The new place we live isn't SOOOOOOOO bad. It's just not the old place, which was, and always will be, the BEST place. Also I have no friends. Even after living here for three whole months.

I rang **Susie** this evening. We talked and she told me everything that was happening at my old school, and it was really nice to hear about everyone, but then she had to go as it was **ROLLER DISCO** night and **Tom** came by for her while we were on the phone. I know if I was there I would have gone too, and I really don't want to feel jealous because I love them both. But I'm not, so I didn't. And I did feel jealous. I asked **Mum** if I could fly over for a couple of laps, but she said only if I had done all my homework, which I obviously hadn't as I had been on the phone with **Susie**.

I miss them.

And **ROLLER DISCOS**.

Everything wouldn't be quite so bad at my new school if **Mrs. Harris** hadn't made one of "**The Populars**" be my "**buddy**"— you know, the person who looks after you and shows you around when you are new in school and have NO FRIENDS.

The other one

Serena

The other other one

You didn't need super vision to see **Serena** make a puking face when **Mrs. Harris** picked her to be my buddy. It's completely humiliating following her around the whole time and knowing that she and the rest of **The Populars** would rather I just disappear.

And how am I supposed to be all friend-makingly funny and witty when I get dragged out in the middle of the night to go on **SUPER** missions?

Hmmmmmm?

We got home at six a.m. and I still had to go to school, which was completely **UNFAIR**. **Mum** said we would be fine if we had a nap. A nap? Aren't they for babies or old people or **dads** on Sundays? As I am none of those, I decided I would NOT nap. That'll show **Mum**.

AFTER SCHOOL . . .

So. Tired. I was so completely exhausted and so happy to get home from school, especially because I accidentally fell asleep in math and dribbled a bit on the desk and now **Serena** hates me more than ever. I was just lying on my bed enjoying staring at the ceiling when **RED** burst in to tell me we were leaving in ten minutes for **Grandma** and **Gramps**'s house. Helpfully, rolling off the bed and hitting the floor woke me up a bit.

We live near **Grandma** and **Gramps** now, and they are the main reason my life has been turned upside down and basically RUINED. **Mum** wanted us to live closer to them so we can help out more, as they are really old. I tried to argue that if we can all fly halfway around the world in under a minute to redirect a baddie's rocket into deep space, then popping over to help **Gramps** lift a car or something should be no problemo. Unsurprisingly, **Mum** wasn't listening, though. But if I have to ruin my life for anyone, I suppose I am glad it is them.

Grandma and Gramps are retired from being **SUPERHEROES** now, and I don't think Grandma misses it one bit, but Gramps always likes to know what's been happening. What I like best about Gramps is that, like RED, one of his superpowers is making fire, from nowhere, out of nothing. He still does it from time to time, but mainly by accident. All you have to do is make him laugh so hard he does a little fart, and that comes out as a tiny fireball. It is HILARIOUS!

Only **Grandma** doesn't think so, as they have gone through a lot of chairs and trousers, and you absolutely CANNOT make him laugh if he is sitting on the posh sofa in the *fancy room.*

Anyway, we lifted the car, had dinner, and it was actually really nice to see **Grandma** and **Gramps**, and I was almost slightly glad we had moved near them UNTIL . . .

. . . The whole way home **RED** just went ON and ON and OOOOOOOOON about her new class and her new friends and being voted onto student council and how she has a special badge and gets to eat cookies at the meetings. It was so totally annoying that if I hadn't been so completely exhausted I would have *zoomed* through the roof of the car to get away from her. Instead, I imagined she was stranded in a laser cage on a planet that is so, so, SOOOOOO far away it doesn't even have a name yet. Which helped.

All that is just typical of **RED**, though. . . . While I'm trailing around after **Serena** and **The Populars** with no friends and no votes and no badges and no cookies, she has managed to completely fit in at school in no time and she doesn't even have to try.

When we FINALLY got home, I went to see BERNARD, and after a brief chat we decided that tomorrow EVERYTHING will change, and I WILL find some actual friends and I WILL get voted to be something and I WILL be a complete success **AND I WILL** have free cookies. Probably. BERNARD the guinea pig squeaked her approval, and we both went to bed.

ZZZzzzzzzzzz.

Well, maybe EVERYTHING hasn't exactly changed yet, as I had planned. I still don't have real friends, and I am not quite a complete success yet. Actually, I haven't even had a cookie, free or otherwise. BUT I have put my name down to be student council representative for my class. I think this is a solid step in the RIGHT direction. If RED can do it, then I am practically certain I can too, and there were only two other names on the list. One was *Sarah Wotton*, who is a complete know-it-all-teacher's-pet-snitch-pants, and the other was RiCKy oWens. I don't believe for one second that he put his own name down, as he is rarely even in class, and when he is, he is not listening. He would definitely not be a good person to represent the needs and concerns of Elephant Class. However, I am an actual superhero, so maybe I might be able to do it? Maybe even be super at it?

I phoned **Tom** about it when I got home and he agrees—student council representative is pretty much in the bag.

VOLUNTEERS FOR STUDENT COUNCIL
Sarah Wotton
Ricky Owenz
Pizazz
DRAMARAMA

BUT THEN . . .

I am not student council representative.

I came in third.

SIGH

ARGH! What a day. Possibly the worst day EVER, and I am no stranger to bad days—take the day I was thrown into an alien snot pit, or the day I was almost squeezed to death by an intergalactic slime worm. And this day definitely was WORSE. . . .

Firstly, *Sarah Wotton* got her student council badge. She would not stop going on about it. And the cookies. Apparently they are really delicious. Whatever.

Secondly, I found I still had gunk in my eyebrows. I found this out by Barry Johnson shouting out very loudly that I had "booger eyebrows."

Thirdly, Serena asked Mrs. Harris, in front of the WHOLE class, if she could not be my buddy anymore as she had been my buddy for AAAAGES and surely I knew where everything was by now.

While I do not have anything in common with **Serena** and **The Populars** and have felt boilingly uncomfortable trailing around after them, at least having her as my buddy gave me a place to be. Without her I will have to wander around on my own AND have to think about where I am wandering, which will be exhausting. And while I agree that **Serena** and I will never actually be for-real buddies, when she asked **Mrs. Harris** if we could unbuddy, well, I haven't felt that embarrassed since I was hit on the head with a **LLAMA** (it's a long story). It is one thing to know that you have no friends at school and probably never will, but it's quite a bit worse to have that confirmed in front of the WHOLE CLASS. *Sarah Wotton* even looked sad for me.

UGH.

Fourthly, **Mrs. Harris** obviously thought that because I put my name down for student council, I actually wanted to do something good for the school instead of just trying to compete with my irritating little sister. Er, actually, **Mrs. Harris**, I do plenty of good things for people all the time—like SAVE THE WORLD. But **Mrs. Harris** clearly decided this was not enough world-saving for one person and has made me *eco monitor* for our class. I don't even get a badge, just a ribbon. A green ribbon. And no cookies. MMMMM'K.

I tried to talk to **Mrs. Harris** about not being *eco monitor*. My old teacher, Mr. Watson, would have known I already save the planet ALL THE TIME. I mean, can't someone else save the planet for a change, please? I explained all this to **Mrs. Harris**, but she just smiled and said that I could use all my planet-saving experience for the job and to give it a go. Then she smiled in a way that told me we would not be discussing it anymore.

ELEPHANT CLASS

ECO MONITOR

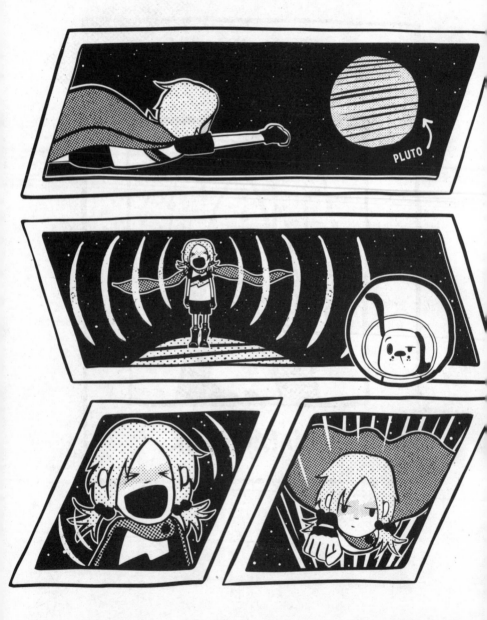

Despite flying to Pluto to let off some steam, I still felt completely wriggly and fully fed up when I got home. I decided I wouldn't actually tell anyone what was wrong because if they really cared they would just know, and gently lure it out of me with hot chocolate and sympathetic looks and pizza. So I went straight to my room and shut the door and decided I would stay there, in my room, on my own, until someone bothered to find out that my life was **STINKY**.

After about fifty hours, **WANDA** came into my room. I didn't think it was because she wanted to gently lure my problems out of me with snacks. **WANDA** confirmed my suspicions by sitting in the middle of my room, sniffing her foot, and then telling me to be ready in one minute as **TWERKNADO** was about to **TWERK A TORNADO!**

Obviously. This was extra annoying as I was rather enjoying my misery and had just gotten halfway through painting my nails black to show everyone how unhappy I was. . . .

Sometimes I wonder why I am not even a little bit popular. I mean, I save the planet and I can fly and I think I have good hair.

Oh yes, AND I am *eco monitor*. Oh well, I guess nobody's perfect. Who knows? Maybe that might even count for something? HAHAHAHAHAAAAAA.

The bit where I decide
to use my eco powers
for good . . .

SUPERHERO STATIONERY!

Well, being *eco monitor* has multiplied the number of people I have spoken to at this school by at least 102, because it turned out there were a LOT of people in my school who all had something to say about how to save the planet. So I figured if I HAD to be *eco monitor*, I may as well get a nice notebook out of it and write down everyone's suggestions in it. Mostly because my memory is STINKY—I think it was irreparably damaged that time I got hit by a **LLAMA** (long story). And also because everybody knows that whether you're superhero-saving the planet or just plain old saving the planet, stationery is KEY.

This meant I had to tell **Mum** everything that had happened when she picked us up from school. It wasn't quite how I wanted her to find out about the millions of things that had been going wrong for me—it really didn't have any of the drama of my original plan (which was to sulk and look sad until I was gently encouraged to talk about it), but I didn't have time for all that now. I needed her to stop at **Pilkingtons** on the way home to get my notebook, because although I am allowed to fly to outer space to defeat evil baddies, I am not allowed to get the bus into town on my own. **AMAZING**.

RED

I was a bit irritated by this missed opportunity for some sympathy snacks, but the thing that REALLY annoyed me was RED being all pleased for me and saying how I would be the BEST *eco monitor* EVER and what a GREAT idea the notebook was and being so super enthusiastic. I don't know why exactly, but it was sooooooo INFURIATING.

Anyway, we did stop at **Pilkingtons** and I got my eco notebook (green and recycled paper, obvs) and RED got a red one. She is super bright and of course completely AWESOME, but has ZERO imagination.

ZERO.

LATER THAT DAY . . .

When I called **Tom** and **Susie** that evening (they were doing homework together at **Susie**'s because it was Wednesday and we always did homework at **Susie**'s on Wednesdays), I tried not to moan too much about the whole *eco monitor* thing as I realized that moaning was all I had done in every single conversation I'd had with them since I left. Like **RED**, they were also really pleased and super enthusiastic about all of it. Unlike **RED**, it wasn't at all annoying when they said it. Hmmmmmm. I started to wonder whether maybe the whole *eco monitor* thing might NOT be the absolute worst thing in the world. Maybe.

All week people came up to me with their planet-saving, environment-mending eco ideas. . . .

PLANET-SAVING

No more homework to save paper and trees.

Save water – never ever wash again. EVER!

Turn off the lights (but only when there's no one in the room).

UGGESTIONS . . .

No more bottled drinks at lunch, and only have refillable water bottles in school.

Recycle all our scrap paper.

SAVE THE TREES and never write in an exercise book again (except this one).

THEN SUDDENLY . . .

. . . Right at the end of the week, a girl from my class called Ivy came over with a suggestion. I mean, she would have an eco suggestion, wouldn't she? She's named after a plant. She told me that some BIG business-type people wanted to **bulldoze** the park next to the school to build a parking lot! She thought that was a VERY bad idea because the trees were actually hundreds and hundreds of years old, and lots of birds and animals lived in the park and it was an extremely pretty and special place right next to the school, and there were loads of parking lots already and why on earth did we need any more and shouldn't we be cycling and walking more ANYWAY?

Then she finished by shoving a newspaper article into my hand that explained the whole thing.

DAILY NEWS

LOCAL PARK UNDER THREAT

CASHCORP set to flatten local park to build ginormous parking lot for loads more cars.

She said all this in a voice that made it sound like it was ALLLLL my fault, which I felt was pretty unfair, but when Ivy told me she had actually WANTED to be *eco monitor*, it made more sense. Apparently she had run the school garden, successfully campaigned for exercise books made from recycled paper, and organized a car pool for the second grade. Then she asked what qualifications was I bringing to the role?

I sort of had to laugh here because she clearly had never heard of my amazing track record for defeating baddies and therefore saving the planet LITERALLY ALL THE TIME!!! Ivy said, well, that's handy and I guess saving a park should be no problem then, should it, and I said, huh, easy peasy lemon squeezy, and she said, great, then turned around and walked away. And THAT is how I decided what my first job as **eco monitor** would be.

I'd show **Ivy** who was saving the world around here. And while I was at it, I could show **RED** and **Mum** and **Dad** and **WANDA** and EVERYONE that although some people might be student council representatives, I—**eco monitor**—was the real mover and shaker around here. Ribbons might even become cooler than badges. I would save the park and everyone would think I was AWESOME! All I had to do was work out how....

FIVE MINUTES LATER . . .

. . . I had thought and thought and thought and thought and still had no ideas, so I decided to do what I always do when a mission is a bit tricky:

ASK **WANDA** . . .

WANDA licked my ear, sniffed the carpet, and then told me that she wasn't authorized to help me with this mission, but she did, however, have a proper super mission from **MISSION CONTROL** and it was very urgent. Apparently uber-baddie GooGoo was having a particularly massive temper tantrum at COT2000—his hilltop hideaway—and was threatening to fire all his toys out of

PRAM1, his super-high-tech tank, onto a small neighboring city, causing devastation, destruction, and a right-old mess.

None of this helped me with saving the park at all, in fact the complete opposite, and I started to tell **WANDA** this . . . but then I looked down and realized she had gone to find the others.

AFTER . . .

It was so good to see **Aunty Blaze**. I think if I had to be anyone in the whole superhero world, it would be **Aunty Blaze**, for these reasons:

Aunty Blaze

She has a good name.

She doesn't have a cape.

She takes no nonsense from anyone, and would not in any way be bothered by **The Populars**.

She's completely awesome and fearless.

Her superpower isn't embarrassing.

Her costume is actually quite cool.

She's always got a plan.

So it made perfect sense to ask **Aunty Blaze** how she would save the park next to the school. . . .

. . . **Mum** butted in and said that while that was the sort of thing we did to baddies on **OFFICIAL SUPERHERO MISSIONS**, that wasn't how it worked normally—in the normal world—like the one most of us live in . . . most of the time. And THIS is exactly the sort of thing **Mum** would say. Yawn. I think she says things like that because **Aunty Blaze** is so successfully super. She's really high up at **MISSION CONTROL** in the **SUPER-SECRET** department and has a really

cool motorbike and "lives life on her terms."
Mum even has to do all her laundry, she's
so successfully super. And cook most of her
meals.

Anyway, then **Mum** did the eyebrow
waggling at **Aunty Blaze**, the thing
grown-ups do at each other that means,
"SHHHHHH, this child will do everything
you say." **Aunty Blaze** then did the "Oh,
right, okay, I'll shut up" face back at **Mum**.
And they think we don't notice! FYI,
grown-ups—kids are not stupid.
Mainly.

And while all this was GREAT, I still had no plan. So I showed them both the article in the newspaper that Ivy gave me and explained VERY CLEARLY that these business types were going to hurt the planet by bulldozing a park to build another parking lot, which would mean more cars, which would hurt the planet even more, and surely that made them big bad baddies and wasn't the whole point of us being **SUPERHEROES** to defeat the baddies however we needed to?

And Aunty Blaze said, "EXACTLY," then pulled the "Oh, right, okay, I'll shut up" face again when Mum glared at her.

Mum said, well, no, bulldozing a park did not seem like a very nice thing to do at all but that the council was probably going to give them permission and that meant you couldn't just barge in and smush their bulldozers, however much you might like to. Because superhero or not, you would probably end up in jail. And Aunty Blaze said I should listen to my mother.

At this point I thought my head might actually explode. I asked **Mum** and ~~Aunty Blaze~~ what was the point of being **SUPER** and saving the stupid world the WHOLE time if the world just kept hurting itself anyway? Amazingly, **Mum** said she actually agreed with me and she thought about it all the time, BUT we all had to remember that superheroes did lots of good things and we had to keep doing good things and hope lots of other people would do good things too, so actually all the good things would outweigh the bad things. She suggested that maybe a good place to start was to talk to the BIG business types, because that is how lots of differences are settled and **blah blah blah**.

Then **RED** backflipped into the room and *blew* the perfect **fireball** and told us she wasn't student council representative anymore, she was now student council **PRESIDENT**.

The bit where it all goes wrong . . .

THE NEXT DAY . . .

I told **Ivy** that my **mum** had suggested we go to the **BIG** business type's offices and just have a nice chat about it. I only said this because I had nothing better to suggest, but surprisingly **Ivy** agreed and thought that maybe if we pointed out how silly the parking lot idea was, they would see sense. We could just remind them that we do **NOT** need more cars, but we do need more trees.

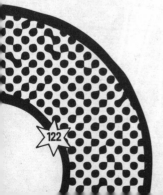

And we could take along some **doughnuts**, because they always help things along. I was not at all sure about this plan as it lacked all the whizzy superhero/world-saving things I am used to, but I DO like doughnuts, so it was decided we would visit the offices of **CASHCORP** after school.

BUT THEN . . .

I am not entirely sure how it could have gone worse, and I didn't even get a sniff of a **doughnut**. It turns out the **BIG CHEESE** at **CASHCORP** was in actual fact **Serena** from **The Populars**'s dad, **Mr. Piffle!**

Once we finally got to see him (a very long story involving a few white lies about a school paper, a smidge of flying, and a tiny bit of sneakiness) we were both a bit frazzled, and in actual fact he doesn't even like **doughnuts**, so they were no help.

Really. Who doesn't like **doughnuts**?

Anyway, standing in front of him and all his MEDIUM TO **LARGE CHEESES** was even more

scary than DABOMB's robot army. At least you know where you stand with a robot army, i.e., they all want to **ZAP** you with their *LASER EYES*. I had no idea what these **CHEESES** were thinking.

As I'm *eco monitor* and therefore in charge, I made **Ivy** do all the talking. And while **Ivy**'s speech was really very informative and she put across a good argument, it didn't really seem to be grabbing the attention of all the different-sized **cheeses**. It felt like it was missing all the *whizziness* of my previous planet-saving, more superhero-type missions, so, quite surprisingly for me, I decided to take ACTION.

Not content with telling us off in person, **Serena**'s dad told on us to **Mrs. Harris**, too, which seemed a bit of an overreaction. I mean, it's not like anyone ended up covered in **radioactive slime** or anything. So then **Mrs. Harris** told us off as well. Well, sort of. I mean, she told us we probably shouldn't have gone to **CASHCORP**'s offices and made

such a mess, and I most likely should not have called Serena's dad a NITWIT. But Mrs. Harris was smiling the whole time, and Ivy and I left feeling very confused as to whether we were actually in trouble or not.

I started to feel that I was making a proper mess of being **eco monitor**. If I am honest, after all my world-saving and facing deadly villains and *zooming* through outer space, I thought saving a park would be a breeze. But it turns out that when your baddies are dressed in suits and they don't use *LASERS* but bits of paper and suitcases, they are much, much harder to defeat.

Serena obviously heard all about it from her **BIG CHEESE** dad and decided to bring it up in study hall in front of the WHOLE CLASS, focusing mainly on the tea cart incident (I only nudged it) and not so much on the bit where I did a perfect somersault over the boardroom table, or even when **Ivy** gave her very good speech. Of course nobody bothered to stop to think about who was actually trying to save the planet and who was being a meany. Instead they all just laughed along with **Serena**'s very one-sided and completely inaccurate retelling of our "meeting."

Sometimes it seems that the less you actually do, the more people think you're great. Take **Serena**, for example. I have to spend my leisure time saving the world for HER. Well, not just for her, obviously, but still, I am running and flying around averting certain doom all over the place and what is she doing? **NOTHING.** But none of that matters because everyone thinks **Serena** is great and I am a loser.

OO UNFAIR...

And why does no one even appreciate
how great MY hair is? I mean it is, isn't it?

The bit where it all goes wrong AGAIN . . .

It just felt like this park-saving was much harder than it should be. I was supposed to be good at this **world-saving** business. It's not like I would ever be able to rely on long division as a fallback, and I'm useless at basketball (I think both are related to the time I got hit on the head with a **LLAMA**— long story), so if I wasn't able to save a teeny bit of green space, what was the point of me? Maybe I just hadn't been super ENOUGH at the meeting. MAYBE it was time to take a bit of Aunty Blaze's advice and go all-out *SUPER*.

If I was SUPER careful, **Mum** would never even have to know.

Yes, it's true. Even superheroes get grounded, and I was most certainly grounded. Literally. I wasn't allowed to fly for a week.

Everyone was furious with me, even Ivy. She said something about it making US look like the baddies rather than **CASHCORP**. This obviously being the exact opposite of what we wanted.

So I had gotten myself in MASSIVE trouble, been grounded, made the only person at school who talks to me FURIOUS, and not helped save the park AT ALL.

Of course Serena had something to say about it too. Right in front of everyone, at dismissal, she made a big thing about how I was just a typical super, *zooming* about making a mess of EVERYTHING, and how I shouldn't be allowed to meddle and . . .

. . . But she didn't get to say anything else because that's when RED stepped in. I don't think I have ever been more pleased to see RED (or actually ever been pleased to see her) and it didn't even occur to me to be irritated that my BABY sister had saved me from Serena. Then she gave me a super-speedy piggyback all the way home.

I called **Susie** and told her I had decided I would resign as *eco monitor* the next morning. **Ivy** would obviously be much better than me. I was clearly no good at being NORMAL and possibly not very good at being **SUPER**. **Susie** said she thought I was actually pretty good at being normal and even really great at being **SUPER**, but just in case, we had a quick brainstorm about what other options I had.

Then **WANDA** padded into my room (without even knocking), rolled around on my homework, knocked over my drink, and told me to get off the phone and come to the kitchen for an **urgent briefing**.

When I got to the kitchen, **RED** gave me one of those "I'm just SO sorry for you" smiles, and it did occur to me to be irritated by my BABY sister.

FACT: those smiles do not help anything and only make you feel cross on top of whatever it is they are sorry about. UGH.

WANDA told us that **CAPTAIN CHAOS** and **Star Slayer** were causing a right old commotion in the outer reaches of the galaxy, and we needed to go and see exactly what they were up to and SHUT. IT. DOWN. This was a HUGE relief, as I had been getting worried about having to be super again after the Mr. Piffle debacle, and although CAPTAIN CHAOS and **Star Slayer** sound scary (and to be fair, they quite often are), they are also KAPOW's mum and dad. I have known KAPOW my WHOLE life, almost. We met in kindergarten and hit it off right away. And even when we realized that he is a supervillain and I am a superhero, we still stayed friends . . . super-secret friends.

THE REST OF THE TIME...

I MEAN, YOU WOULD IF YOU COULD, WOULDN'T YOU?

EYE ROLL

IT TURNS OUT THAT KAPOW AND I BOTH FEEL THE SAME WAY ABOUT BEING **SUPER**. AS YOU KNOW, I AM REALLY NOT AT ALL SURE ABOUT BEING A **SUPERHERO**, AND KAPOW IS NOT AT ALL KEEN ON BEING A **SUPERVILLAIN**. THIS MEANS THAT WHENEVER WE MEET UP TO FIGHT IT OUT, KAPOW AND I USUALLY JUST PRETEND, WRESTLE, THEN SNEAK OFF FOR A CHAT. **THIS MISSION WAS NO DIFFERENT...**

First thing, I asked **Ivy** what she thought we should do to save the park. I got a very strong feeling **Ivy** had been preparing for this moment, which made me feel even worse for not asking sooner.

Ivy thought we should organize a few of us to hold a protest by the entrance to the park after school on Friday. So when all the parents came to collect their children from school, they could see what was going on, and then they would want to save the park too.

While I thought this seemed like a NICE idea, it didn't really feel like it had any of the punch of our first two tries. How would standing around and just chatting to people save anything? I started to say as much to **Ivy**, but then I remembered **KAPOW**'s EYE ROLL and how my attempts at park-saving had worked out, and so instead of telling **Ivy** her idea was weak, I asked if she wanted to come over for dinner so we could make a plan for Friday.

And amazingly, she said yes!

School seemed to go on forever, and 𝕊erena really didn't miss a single chance to tease me allll day. . . .

AT LUNCH

EVEN DURING PE!

. . . But by the end of the day I had sort of zoned out and couldn't really hear her anymore. It's a survival trick I learned from living with R E D and her going on and on and on and on about EVERYTHING, ✷

ALL

THE

TIME.

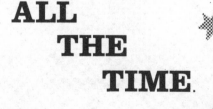

155

The bell for dismissal rang, and I met Ivy at the school gates. We walked home because I was still grounded (for anything other than planetary emergencies) and Ivy can't fly, obviously, so it took aaaages, but it did give us a chance to chat about our **park protest**. We made up a sort of songy chant thing we could sing to get people's attention. I had never had to sing/chant to save the planet before, and I wondered if maybe this could be my signature **SUPERHERO** move—instead of my completely embarrassing, humiliating one that I still don't want to talk about. Then Ivy asked what we would have for dinner, and I think she was a bit disappointed when I said spaghetti. I am not sure what she thought supers ate, but she was obviously hoping for something more exciting than spaghetti.

I wish!

When we got home we told **Mum** all about our idea, and she said it sounded great and that we should probably go and speak to **Gramps** because he had done a little bit of protesting, himself, back in the day.

So we did. **Mum** even drove us over while **Dad** made tea. **Gramps** and **Grandma** were very pleased to see us, and **Grandma** asked if I had explained the not-making-**Gramps**-laugh rule to **Ivy** and I hadn't, so I did, but this made **Ivy** laugh, which made **Gramps** laugh, which made all of us laugh, and this made **Gramps** laugh even more and before you knew it, he let out a fart, and **Grandma** was putting out a flaming throw pillow with her handy handbag-sized fire extinguisher.

We decided to go outside and walk around the garden in case of any more little "fireballs," and **Gramps** told us all about his protest. Apparently, an **ANGRY SHOUTY MAN** started telling anyone who would listen that supers were different, and not like normal people, which is sort of true, but then he said that's why they couldn't be trusted, as they would only use their **SUPER**powers for themselves. And because of that he said supers should go and live far away from everyone else and STAY AWAY. And some people started to listen to him because, well, he was angrily shouting

VERY
LOUDLY.

Obviously **Gramps** didn't agree with what the **ANGRY SHOUTY MAN** was saying for lots of reasons—the main one being that supers were only being super to protect **EVERYONE IN THE WHOLE WORLD, EVEN THE WHOLE UNIVERSE**, and actually, they were much more like normal people than they were different from them. They could just fly and stuff, too.

Firstly, it made **Gramps** cross (which I could NOT imagine), and he wanted to whizz around the planet a million times to turn back time and stop the **ANGRY SHOUTY MAN** before he started shouting or even got angry. Then he thought he might like to push the **ANGRY SHOUTY MAN** into deepest space so the man could see how he liked it out on his own, but then **Gramps** finally calmed down and realized that these ideas were not very nice at all, and that using his **SUPER**powers to try to solve this problem would only make things worse.

People would only see how different he was from them, not how he was the same, and that was exactly what the **ANGRY SHOUTY MAN** wanted. **Gramps** realized he could only really fix this problem by being everyday super. Not **SUPER** super. So he went to the garage and used some old wood and a stick (which he thought must have been left there by the people who lived there before, because he did NOT do DIY), and he used them to make a sign. Then off he went to where the **ANGRY SHOUTY MAN** was angrily shouting, and he started to calmly protest. He even made up a song, too.

It turned out lots of other people agreed with **Gramps**, and some of them joined in. First it was mainly other supers, but slowly all kinds of people got involved. And the more people got involved, the more people noticed, and eventually the **ANGRY SHOUTY MAN** couldn't shout above everyone else's singing, so he shut up and went away (even though no one had told him to).

So that was that. Well, until the next time, **Gramps** said.

Then **Gramps** took me and Ivy to the garage, where there was lots of old wood and sticks (because when he made that first sign, he realized he actually LOVED DIY), and we made some signs for our park protest. It felt totally weird not to just *whizz* off and use my embarrassing superpower to save the day, but instead I got to hang out with **Gramps** and Ivy in the garage, chatting and painting and hammering. I wondered if this really could actually make a difference, and I

wasn't at all sure it could, as it was all just too, well, normal, but it was also very nice, so I did it anyway. Ivy said the signs looked really good, and **Gramps** seemed very pleased about this and said he couldn't be happier, as he'd thought his planet-saving days were over. Then **Grandma** brought us all some chips and cookies and I thought how much nicer other planet-saving missions would be if they involved more **snacks**.

At school the next day Ivy and I drew some leaflets to hand out at the protest, and we photocopied them in the library. (Mr. Simpson, the librarian, thought it was a great idea, as he ate his lunch in the park every day, AND he said he would come along on Friday to support the protest.)

SAVE OUR PARK!!!

Our lovely park is UNDER THREAT!

We want parks, NOT CARS!!!

Please come and help us save our park.

WHEN? This Friday, after school

WHERE? THE PARK (next to school)

WHY? Because it is lovely and there are lots of animals living there and it belongs to US!!!

THE BIG DAY ARRIVED . . .

I woke up on Friday with 𝓑𝓤𝓑𝓑𝓛𝓔𝓢 in my tummy, and this was extremely weird, as all I was going to do was stand around with a sign. It's not like I had to fly off into deepest **darkest** space to stop an alien overlord or anything. All my classes took forever, and Ivy and I could barely eat any lunch at all. I think her tummy had 𝓑𝓤𝓑𝓑𝓛𝓔𝓢 too. And then ALL OF A SUDDEN it was dismissal. . . .

Gramps was outside school with the signs as we had arranged, and we picked them up, stood by the park, and started our chant. It all felt a bit silly at first, just me, Ivy, and

Gramps chanting away, and people trying to chat over the top. I felt like I should DO something **SUPER** to get things moving. But then I remembered where that had gotten me before, and I really did want to save the park this time, so I just kept going.

Molly and Ed, **Ivy**'s friends, met us and joined in, then the librarian, Mr. Simpson, came along, and then even **Mrs. Harris**. **Serena** looked at us like we smelled funny and started calling someone on the phone that she is absolutely not allowed to take to school.

RED brought the student council along, and I thought, UGH, TYPICAL, I can't even have a protest without her butting in. But then they all set up a **LEMONADE** stall just by the entrance to the park, and people actually seemed to like that a lot, and even took their **LEMONADE** into the park, and it felt like although nothing was really happening, something was sort of happening, and that something was hopefully a good thing.

FREE LEMONADE!

FREE LEMONADE!

We handed out our leaflets. Molly had even started a petition for people to sign. And they did! We kept singing and chanting and waving our signs about. Then **Mum** came down with **Grandma** and **WANDA**, and I thought how nice that was until it was actually completely awful because right in the middle of our protest, **WANDA** piped up with an **URGENT MISSION**. I looked at **Mum**, who

just shrugged her shoulders and did the "I'm sorry" smile, which still didn't help. I thought **Ivy** would hate me because just like always, right in the middle of the best thing I have done in ages, I had to *zoom off* for a mission. And it was gross **big baddie MEGAVOM**, and those **missions never ended well**.

KEEP OUR PARK GREEN KEEP THE PLANET CLEAN!

ROOOOAAR!!!

RUMBLE!   RUMBLE!

I *zoomed* back to the park as fast as I could, which fortunately *whizzed* most of the puke off me, but I still landed in a panic. I didn't have to worry, though, because Gramps and Ivy were laughing (but not quite enough for a fireball—phew) and everything seemed okay. Ivy said they had held the fort just fine, and there was even a whisper going around that the local newspaper was going to come along. Oh, and the student council had run out of LEMONADE and wasn't it great that people seemed to actually care about this little park after all and . . .

Well, I'll never know what she was going to say next because I couldn't hear Ivy over the **ROAR** of a bulldozer. And the **ROAR** of Mr. Piffle on the bulldozer.

The action-packed bit

(where I have to use my stupid superpower)...

Mr. Piffle *zoomed* *up* to the park. Well, I say *zoomed*—bulldozers don't actually go that fast, so it took him quite a while, and it was a bit embarrassing, but when he did make it to the park entrance, he was LIVID, and a sort of purply color.

Purple Mr. Piffle stopped the bulldozer because it was really quite hard to hear him over the top of the racket it was making. Then he looked down on us and told us we were all standing in the way of progress, literally. We should stop being silly because of course we needed more space to park more cars and what was the point of a tiny, scruffy park anyway? And we should not concern ourselves with the business of **BIG** business, and we should just let the **BIG** businessmen get on with it because after all, they knew what was best and we should also GET OUT OF THE WAAAAAY.

Then **Ivy** did something extremely brave and stepped forward, and very politely and not at all shoutily, she pointed out to **Mr. Piffle** that people were enjoying their little park and why would he want to take that away, and anyway, just how much money were he and **CASHCORP** going to make out of squishing our park and building their parking lot? Amazingly, **Mr. Piffle** went even more purple and managed to look even more angry, which I did not believe was possible until I saw him do it. If he was **SUPER**, that would for sure be his **SUPER**power.

Mr. Piffle started up his bulldozer again and headed toward the park entrance. I was quite sure all the briefcases and bits of paper in the world did not mean he could just drive through our protest and squash the park without proper permission or anything. Everyone sort of panicked a bit, and Ivy looked really sad. It seemed such a shame that just as everyone realized how much they liked the little park, Mr. Piffle was going to squash it anyway. We had to stop him.

But how?

I looked at **Mum**, who nodded and mouthed, "Go ON!" (I mean, she might have actually said it, but the bulldozer made it impossible to tell.) Then I looked at **WANDA**, who sniffed a flower, scratched her ear, and nodded too. Even **Gramps** gave me a shove. And then I looked at Ivy. I had messed things up so many times trying to be **SUPER**, and I wanted to make a friend as well as save the little park, but Ivy just looked so sad and I knew I had to do something. The most embarrassing thing, the thing I tried so hard all the time NOT to do. But here I was about to do it in front of EVERYONE at school, slightly covered in vomit. . . .

I would have to use my SUPERPOWER.

SLOWLY, A GLITTER STORM APPEARED IN FRONT OF ME, AND I USED THAT GLITTER STORM (I CAN CONTROL IT WITH MY JAZZ HANDS—I KNOW!) TO PUSH THE BULLDOZER BACK ONTO THE ROAD AND AWAY FROM THE LITTLE PARK.

Well, this made **Mr. Piffle**
properly angry, and he
jumped down from his
now very sparkly
bulldozer and started yelling
right in the protesters' faces.
All this happened just as the local
paper turned up and took lots of photos
of him **screaming**. This seemed to
make him even more angry, and then
everyone started booing and **Serena**
and **The Populars** disappeared and
Mr. Piffle looked extremely bothered,
made a very strange angry gargling
noise, and stomped off, leaving his
DISCO bulldozer right in the middle
of the road! I used my jazz
hands/glitter storm
and carefully moved
it to the side

of the road so everyone could go home. (I mean, everyone had seen my embarrassing **SUPERPOWER** at this point, so WHATEVER.) But then the best thing happened. No one (well, almost no one) went home. Everyone cheered and stayed in the park, and **RED** used her super speed to whip up some more **LEMONADE**, and then the ice-cream truck turned up and it was really, **REALLY** super.

The end bit . . .

. . . or is it?

Yes . . .

. . . or is it?

It turned out that because **Mr. Piffle** hadn't gotten permission yet to squish the park, he was now in BIG TROUBLE, and **Serena** was extremely quiet about that, but she was less quiet about my embarrassing **SUPERPOWER** and teases me about it whenever she can.

But do you know what? I don't even mind that much, because now I have a friend at school, one who actually thinks my **SUPERPOWER** is pretty cool. I KNOW! In fact, I have three friends—**Ivy**, **Molly**, and **Ed**, or the eco council, as we are otherwise known. We hold regular council meetings in the park, and **Tom** and **Susie** even came along

to one of them. Well, it was more of a picnic than a meeting, but it was great all the same. And as I looked around at our slightly less-scruffy-looking park (**Gramps** now heads up a volunteer group who is making it pretty special—I guess **he just can't stop saving the planet!**), I realized that no matter how much I might not want to ALWAYS save the planet (and sometimes it seems like there is just too much to do), I am always glad when I have. One bit at a time. So far we haven't had to protest again, but **Gramps** said the garage is ready if we do.

And now you know. That's my *SUPER SUPERPOWER*. Not kung fu, not LASER EYES, not even supersonic projectile vomiting. No, my *SUPERPOWER* is **jazz hands**. Jazz hands that then create a glitter* storm that I can move at my will. And, yes, it is COMPLETELY EMBARRASSING.

*biodegradable, obviously!

TA-DAH

I guess now you know
why I am called
Pizazz.

TO BE CONTINUED . . .

Look out for
Pizazz's
next **SUPER**
adventure!